GREEN & GROOVY CRAFTS

GARBAGE FLOWERS™

by Eric Lewis

PRINTED ON
RECYCLED
PAPER

TURN TRASH
INTO COOL
TREASURES

GREEN & GROOVY CRAFTS

GARBAGE FLOWERS™

by Eric Lewis

Illustrations by
Eric Lewis

Photographs by
Aydin Arjomand

downtown bookworks

downtown bookworks

Designed by Georgia Rucker Design
Typeset in CCDigital Delivery and Soap

Printed in China
February 2011

ISBN 978-1-935-703-16-7

10 9 8 7 6 5 4 3 2 1

Downtown Bookworks Inc.
285 West Broadway
New York, NY 10013
www.downtownbookworks.com

Note: With any craft project, check product labels to make sure that the
materials you use are safe and nontoxic.

CONTENTS

THE ORIGINAL Seeds

O nce upon a time, I was a student at the Rhode Island School of Design. While there, in September of 2003, I began what became an ongoing recycled design project, *Saved By Eric*. I was inspired by the recycled design of non-industrialized nations, as well as by artists like Marcel Duchamp (the guy who came up with *readymades*—don't know what they are? Read the next page!) and Andy Warhol (famous for turning Brillo® boxes into art). *Saved By Eric*'s goal is to practice "recognizably recycled design" by making objects out of environmental waste that keep as much of their original identity as trash as possible. I am always on a quest for *maximum transformation* from *minimum alteration*.

Garbage Flower No. 1 blossomed out of an enormous pile of junk in my living room. That original seed was a 1930s cast-iron metal cart wheel. Many more Garbage Flowers grew from my living room dump—things that were too small to be appreciated as larger readymades (Did you skip ahead to read about readymades? Well, what are you waiting for?) A dryer knob, a small doll's head, a flattened soda can, the top half of a plastic soda bottle, and even an old light bulb were all early Garbage Flower blooms.

Unlike regular flowers, Garbage Flowers do not die. Part of what is so unique about them is that the concept

The original!

CONE VASE

works for so many kinds of junk—they really encourage us to look at previously disposable stuff in a new and different light. They take the utter chaos of a pile of garbage and give it order—make it possible to plant it in rows. And making them is so simple! A piece of wire, a green label, and suddenly you have a way to appreciate the beauty of something that would otherwise have been too boring or broken to be noticed. Garbage Flowers are not exclusive to plastic rejects from the toy bin. Kitchen utensil drawers, desktops, and the garage tool bench are great places to look for Garbage Flower blooms.

Garbage Flowers and Readymades

Readymades are manufactured objects, such as a snow shovel or a comb, selected by the artist, titled, signed, and called "art." Marcel Duchamp came up with the idea of readymades in 1913 with a work called *Bicycle Wheel*. It consisted of a bicycle wheel mounted on top of a stool. Because he slightly altered the manufactured objects to create this, he called it an "assisted readymade." One year later, he created the first "pure readymade," an object completely unaltered by the artist except for giving it a name and signing it. It was a bottle-drying rack, and he titled it *Hedgehog* (1914).

Marcel Duchamp's *Bicycle Wheel*

Duchamp's most famous readymade was a urinal that he titled *Fountain* (1917). Back then, the idea of an "already made" work of art was so shocking *Fountain* was rejected from an art exhibit that accepted all entries! Today, however, many art experts agree that it is one of the most important works of the 20th century.

Because Garbage Flowers are made by attaching trash along with paper leaves to wire stems, I like to think of them as small assisted readymades. Are they art? I think so.

Marcel Duchamp's *Fountain* as Garbage Flower

lewis

WHAT'S IN HERE?

We're providing you with the wire and the pliers that you will use throughout the book. (If you run out of kit wire you can easily get more 15-gauge wire at your local craft or hardware store.) It will be up to you to provide your own flower "bud" materials. Don't worry if your creations don't look exactly like ours. Yours will depend on the refuse you not only find most appealing but that lends itself most readily to your Garbage Flower technique. Physics do play a part in constructing a Garbage Flower (see page 18). Start out with things that are more straightforward like bottles and light bulbs. Then move on to heavier or more complicated items like plastic toys and costume jewelry. Don't be discouraged—your Garbage Flowers will have their own personalities. No need to stick to our designs—let your creativity flow and your gardens will take off on their own.

Make YOUR OWN Leaves

If you run out of the leaf labels provided in this book or just want to make your own, it is easy. They can be made out of old comic books, empty cereal boxes, or just about any piece of paper or cardboard that would otherwise be thrown away. You will also need a pair of scissors and tape, preferably anything stronger than the standard clear stuff. Duct tape is the best; in a pinch, even masking tape will work.

1. Cut a 2-inch by 1-inch rectangle of tape from the roll.

2. Cut two crescent shapes into the sides of the tape—one on top, another directly below it. You can draw the crescent shapes first to make sure they are somewhat equal in size.

3. Place the piece of tape on a flat surface, adhesive side UP, and place your stem right in the middle of the crescent shapes. Place the piece of paper or cardboard you will be turning into a leaf on the right edge of the crescent shape, sticking it to the tape. Then fold the left side of the piece of tape over the stem and onto the top of your leaf.

STEM

COMIC STRIP

4. Using scissors, trim the piece of paper or cardboard into a leaf shape.

How to PLANT
GARBAGE FLOWERS

The world is your flowerbed when it comes to the best items to use as Garbage Flower containers. Most successful items will be variations on one of two themes: 1) some form of container tightly packed with Styrofoam (or filled with weights like marbles); 2) a container with holes the right size for the wire to pass through.

TOMATO PASTE CAN

COFFEE CAN

Look For Items Like These:

OATMEAL CAN

COFFEE CAN

SOUP CAN

TOMATO PASTE CAN

VINTAGE TINS

CHEESE GRATER

COLANDER

STYROFOAM SHAPES

TERRACOTTA POT

WINE BOTTLE CRATE

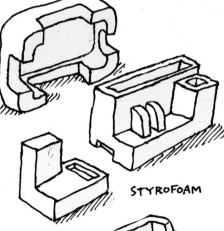

STYROFOAM

CHEESE GRATER

MASON JAR

MARBLES

SOUP CAN

HOW TO GROW A BOTTLE FLOWER:

The original eleven-step process explained

1. FIND A BOTTLE.

Choose the disposable plastic bottle in a size and color you like.

2. PUNCTURE IT.

Use a kitchen knife or a craft knife to pierce the top third of the bottle. Be careful when making the cut! Start a slash long enough to insert a scissor blade; this makes the next step easier. If the scissors are sharp enough and the plastic bottle thin enough, the scissors may be used to puncture the bottle.

3. CUT THE TOP.

Using regular scissors, cut off the top section of the bottle.

you'll have a piece that looks something like this.

4. CHOOSE A WIRE STEM.

Use one of the pre-cut wire stems that comes with this kit. Or, measure an 18-inch length of 15-gauge wire easily found at craft and hardware stores. Holding on with the pliers, wiggle the measured length back and forth with your free hand until it breaks free from the coil. Sharp scissors should also snip this wire.

5. STRAIGHTEN THE STEM.

Use your fingers to smooth out the kinks or bends in the wire stem.

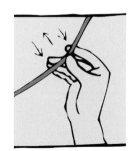

When you are done, the stem should look like this.

6. WRAP THE WIRE.
Wrap one end of the wire around the bottle's neck as tightly as possible, overlapping the end on the longer stem section and twisting to secure.

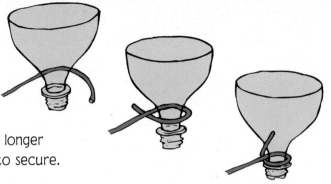

7. BEND THE STEM.
Use the pliers to hold the short end of the wire and use your free hand to bend the rest of the wire down against the bottle's neck.

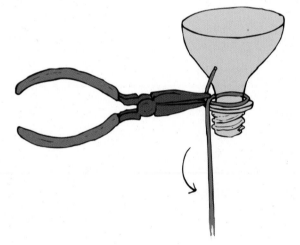

8. BEND IT AGAIN.
Grasp the wire with the pliers, right at the bottle's neck, and, with your hand, bend the stem across the opening. Bend it flush with the opening—the tighter, the better!

Your garbage flower should now look like this. →

9. NOW BEND IT ONCE MORE. With the pliers, grasp the wire right in the middle of the bottle's opening. Use your free hand to bend the stem away from the opening, at a right angle — the stem should look like it is coming straight out of the bottle.

Voilà! Your garbage flower is almost complete! →

10. ADD A LEAF. Remove the leaf from its backing (if you are using the sticky ones that come with this book). Place the leaf, adhesive side up, on a flat surface. Lay the wire stem across the narrow middle of the leaf. Gently lift one side of the leaf and press it against the stem to adhere; then fold it all the way over the stem, aligning it with the other side. Press the two sides together. Pinch the leaf right at the stem to secure. For instructions on how to make your own leaves, see page 6.

11. TA-DA! Don't forget to sign your art! Use a permanent marker to sign the leaf or write a brief description of where it you found your flower or another meaningful inscription.

HOW TO GROW
A Light Bulb Flower

Apart from the fact that the bulb should have outlived its usefulness as an actual light source, pretty much any light bulb will make an interesting garbage flower. Grouped together, they shed a creative glow anywhere you plant them.

1. **FIND a BURNED-OUT LIGHT BULB.** They come in all shapes and sizes, most of them in frosted or clear glass. Colors work well too.

2. CHOOSE a WIRE STEM.
Use one of the pre-cut wire stems that comes with this kit. Or, measure an 18-inch length of 15-gauge wire easily found at craft and hardware stores. Holding on with the pliers, wiggle the measured length back and forth with your free hand until it breaks free from the coil. Sharp scissors should also snip this wire.

3. STRAIGHTEN THE STEM.
Use your fingers to smooth out the kinks or bends in the wire stem.

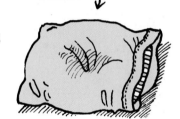

When you are done, the stem should look like this.

4. FIND a PILLOW.
Find a pillow to use as a work surface. Working over a pillow will help keep the bulb from shattering.

PILLOW ↴

5. MAKE a LOOP aT ONE END OF THE STEM.
A good way to begin the loop is to wrap one end of the stem around the metal base of the bulb. Then, make the loop slightly smaller than the diameter of the bulb's metal base by gently tugging the ends in opposite directions, using the pliers to grab the shorter end.

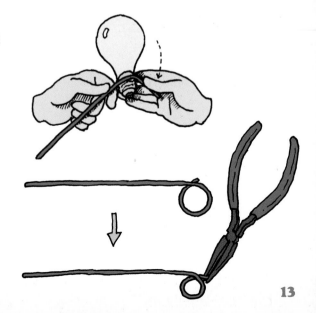

6. SCREW YOUR BULB INTO THE LOOP.

Use your fingers to gently widen the loop until the bulb's metal base fits inside it. Once the screw threads have engaged with the stem, turn the bulb clockwise until the tip of the base is completely screwed through the loop.

Your Garbage Flower should now look like this.

7. BEND THE STEM.

Use the pliers to hold the wire where it meets the bulb and bend the stem down with your free hand.

8. BEND IT AGAIN.

Now grasp the stem with the pliers, right at the tip of the metal base and, with your free hand, bend the stem across the pointy tip of the bulb's base.

9. **now Bend IT once MoRe.** With the pliers, grasp the stem directly under the pointy tip of the metal base. Use your free hand to bend the stem away from the metal tip, at a right angle.

10. **aDD a LeaF.** Remove the leaf from its backing (if you are using the adhesive ones that come with this book). Place the leaf, adhesive side up, on a flat surface. Lay the wire stem across the narrow middle of the leaf as shown. Gently lift one side of the leaf and press it against the stem to adhere; then fold it all the way over the stem, aligning it with the other side. Press the two sides together. Pinch the leaf right at the stem to secure. For instructions on how to make your own leaves, see page 6.

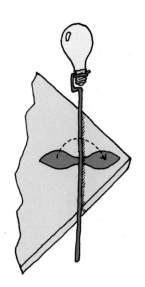

11. **VOILà!** Don't forget to sign you're your art! Use a permanent marker to sign the leaf or write a brief description of where it you found your flower or another meaningful inscription.

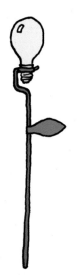

HOW TO MAKE A PLASTIC TOY GARBAGE FLOWER

The final hurrah for everything from construction toy parts to discarded kiddie-meal toys and from abandoned superheroes to disconnected doll heads. Unlike GFs made from bottles and bulbs, every Garbage Flower that uses a plastic toy will employ a slightly different wire-wrapping technique. You'll need to take into account the weight of the object vs. the length of the stem (so the stem doesn't bend too much).

1. FIND a TOY. Because plastic toys come in such a wide variety of shapes, there is no single way to attach a Garbage Flower stem. However, there are a few basic methods that will be helpful when turning toys into flowers.

2. ACTION FIGURE/DOLL

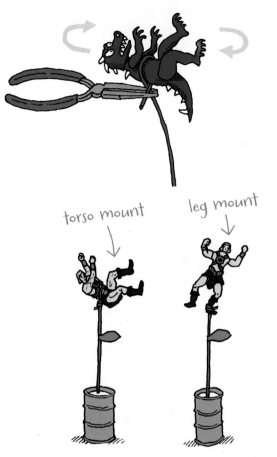

Wrap one end of the stem around the waist of your toy. While using the pliers to hold both ends of the wire loop together, gently twist your toy around a couple of times, tightening the loop.

I like wrapping the stem around an action figure's waist because the arms and legs of the figure can behave like petals, which you can adjust to your liking. However, you may decide that you want He-Man to stand tall in your bouquet, victorious over the other flowers. In this case, a leg-mounted stem attachment is preferable. Decisions like this are entirely up to you and are part of the fun of making Garbage Flowers.

torso mount

leg mount

3. TAKE ADVANTAGE OF THE HOLE IN A PLASTIC TOY.

Many plastic toys have holes in them, often where a deeply-set screw attaches two different parts. If the hole is deep enough, try this method. Using the pliers, bend one end of the stem into a sharp upside-down v-shape. Make sure the width of your V is wider than the width of the hole. Insert upside-down V into the hole, and push hard.

THE PHYSICS OF GARBAGE FLOWERS OR 3 GREEN THUMB GRAVITATIONAL PROPERTIES

From plastic toys to kitchen gadgets to broken bits of hardware you find in the garage, the oddest shaped items make the most intriguing Garbage Flowers. However, it pays to keep certain physical properties in mind as you create GFs out of funky stuff. Think of these things as "Green Thumb Gravitational Properties."

GREEN THUMB GRAVITATIONAL PROPERTY NO. 1: WEIGHT

The most important factor in deciding whether a piece of junk can become a Garbage Flower is its weight. If the item is too heavy, the stem will not be strong enough to keep it aloft. This is why lightweight objects like plastic soda bottles and lightbulbs are so well suited to transformation. There is however, a bit of wiggle room in this law; the shorter the wire stem, the more weight it will be able to support. So, if you have attached a heavyish object to your stem and it keeps flopping over when you plant it, try shortening the stem (see cell-phone flower drawing). You can keep shortening the stem until it retains enough rigidity, but at a certain point, you may have to decide that the object just wasn't meant to become a flower.

GReen THUMB GRavITaTIONaL PROPERTY NO. 2: SIZE

Another important consideration is the size of the blossom. It shouldn't be too big or too small. The perfect approximate size for a Garbage Flower blossom is a 3-inch by 3-inch by 3-inch cube or a ball with a 3-inch diameter. Much bigger, and it will probably be too heavy, but more importantly, it stops looking like a flower—the stem, juxtaposed against such a big object will seem to disappear, and you'll be left with a mysterious, floating-garbage thingy. Much smaller than a 3-inch ball, and the opposite happens—the stem is visually over-emphasized, and one wonders why so much trouble was expended to attach such a teensy thing to a seemingly giant stem. (See page 40 for Bonsai [aka mini] Garbage Flowers with ideas for how to make arrangements of smaller flowers.)

GReen THUMB GRavITaTIONaL PROPERTY NO. 3:

No matter the weight, size, or shape of your blossoms, it is always important to attach the object as tightly as possible to your wire stem. You don't want your blossom to wiggle around at the top of the stem. You can check for this by holding your newly constructed flower by the stem, an inch or so below the blossom, and give it a little jostle. The blossom should not budge!

WEIGHT ISSUE

Cell phone with stem too long

Stem length correct for cell phone

PLANT a BOTTLE FLOWER GARDEN

ALL sorts of curiously shaped and colored plastic bottles (not to mention the odd spray nozzle) make fantastic garbage flowers. The basic steps are always the same, but the results are wildly varied.

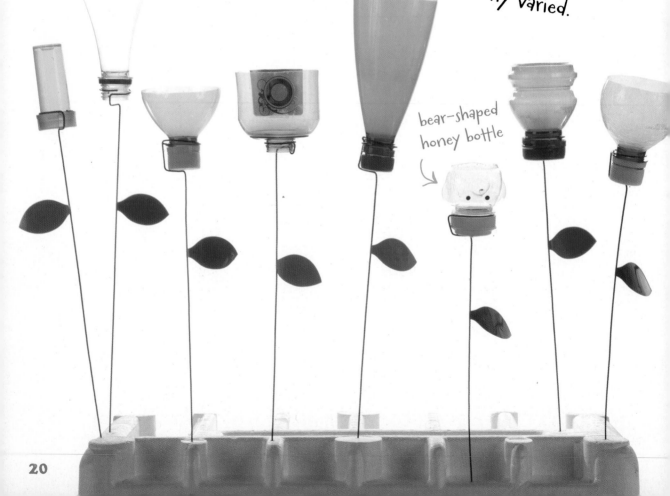

bear-shaped honey bottle

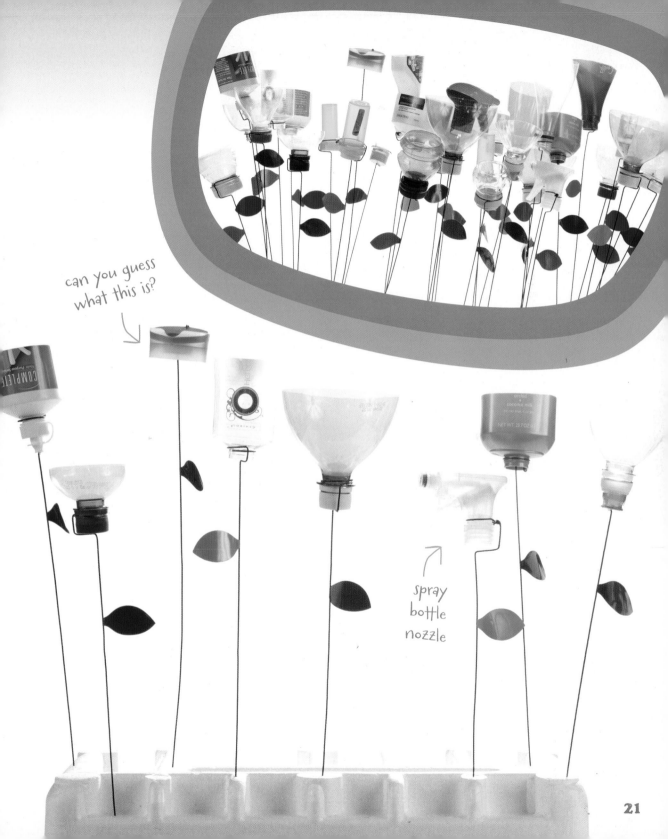

can you guess
what this is?

spray
bottle
nozzle

PLANT A LIGHT BULB

Get creative in your search for burned-out bulbs. There is no end to the odd shapes, sizes, and colors you'll discover, opening a world of possibilities for beautiful bulb bouquets.

FLOWer Garden

PLANT A mixeD-uP GARDEN

The Garbage Flower equivalent of the mixed-seed packet, this garden has everything plus the kitchen sink.

eye glasses

?

keys

light
switch

plastic
bookshelf
connector

contact
lens case

toilet
flush
knob

PLANT A PLASTIC TOY
FLOWER GARDEN

Making Garbage Flowers is a whimsical way to give new life to the world of small plastic things, be they shaped like humans, animals, robots, aliens, or something in between.

rescued in Central Park

yo-yo

hamster
house piece

GIVE THE GIFT OF
GARBAGE FLOWERS

Does someone you know love to cook? Whip up a Garbage Flower bouquet, using kitchen thing-a-ma-bobs for flower tops. Music, art, sports, or cars more your speed? Create a Garbage Flower bouquet in which all the flowers relate to a particular passion or hobby. These 3-D greeting cards make really cool gifts.

tea strainer

cookie cutter

oven knob

salt shaker

carrot peeler

oven thermometer

DELICIOSO!

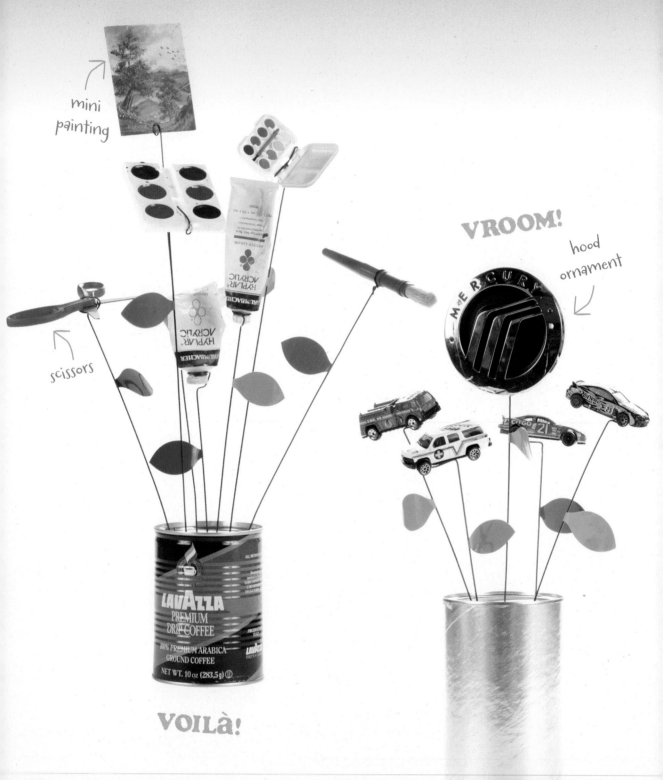

mini painting

scissors

VROOM!

hood ornament

VOILÀ!

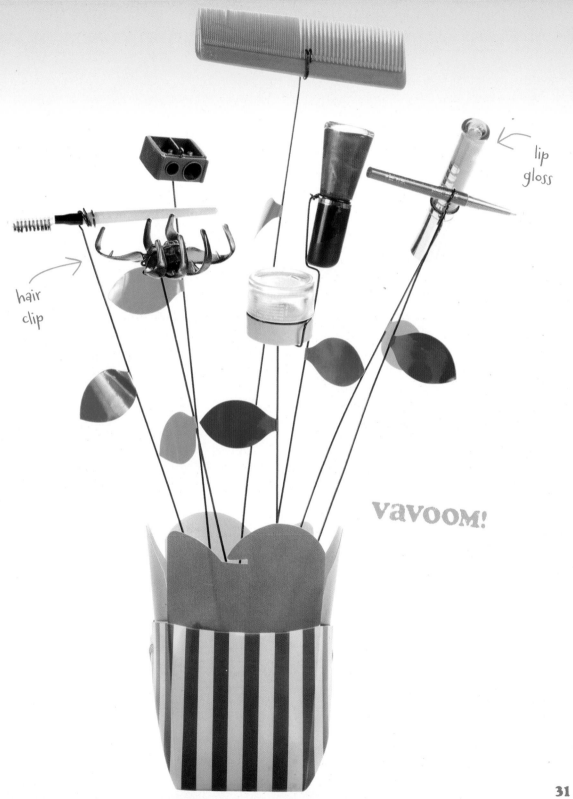

lip
gloss

hair
clip

vavoom!

half a swim goggle

trophy top

SCORe!

encore!

stereo
knob

turntable
tonearm

headphones

FORE!

GROW a techno...

Round up your old, out-of-date technical stuff—cordless phones, dead laptops, fried computer towers, etc.—and look inside to make tech-tastic Garbage Flowers. Used-up motherboards or other electronic innards make really cool Garbage Flowers.

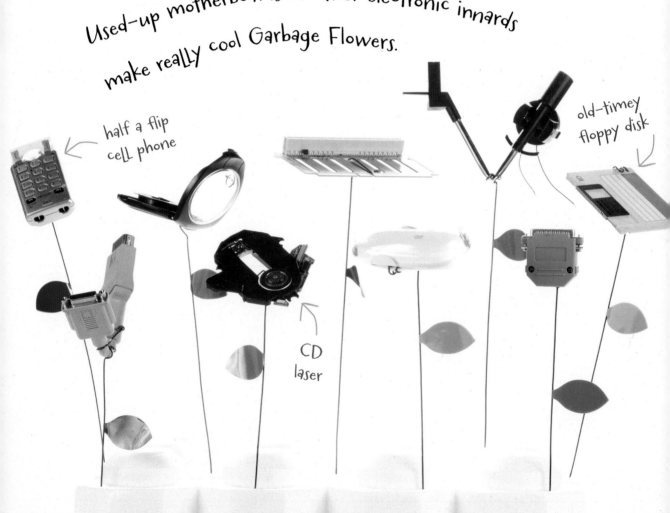

half a flip cell phone

old-timey floppy disk

CD laser

tANiCAL GARDEN

piece of computer motherboard

the other half

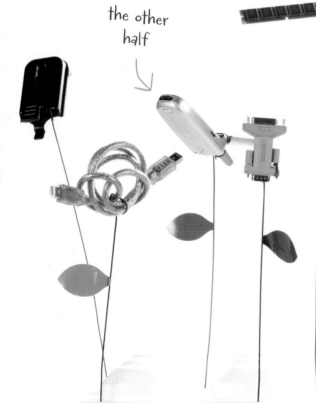

antique remote control

PETAL POWER
GARBAGE FLOWER POTS

Don't forget that happiest of coincidences, a Flower Garbage Flower, or a GF that started life as one odd thing or another, but once attached to the end of a wire stem, does a mean imitation of an actual blossom. Water spigot knobs, plastic fan blades, and badminton birdies are just a few of the items that look as much like posies plucked from the nearest garden as they do themselves.

badminton birdie

candle wax catcher

fan blade

cookie cutter $\rightarrow$

crystal
chandelier
thingy $\leftarrow$

spigot knob

CELEBRATE!
WITH GARBAGE FLOWERS

Name the celebration—birthday, new baby, first day of school, graduation, or congratulations on your new job—and there is a Garbage Flower bouquet waiting in the wings to help get the party started.

sippy cup top

baby fork

GET WELL SOON!

pill bottle

first aid tape

baby food jar

HAPPY new BABY!

tree
ornament

gift
topper

**an eco-FRIENDLY alternative
TO a CHRISTMAS TREE**

CULTIVATE BONSAI (aka MINI) GARBAGE FLOWERS

They may be small, but boy-oh-boy are they ever cute. Stems from paper clips, poked into pink erasers, or teeny tea tins, they are the bonsais of the genus Garbage Flower.

HOW TO MAKE STEMS FOR BONSAI GARBAGE FLOWERS:

1. Find a paper clip, preferably a medium-to-large-size one, either metal or color-coated.

2. Using your pliers, straighten the three bends in the paper clip until you have a straight length of wire.

3. Attaching the stem depends on what your bonsai blossom is, but it often helps to make a small loop on one end of the paper clip, place it around your item, and then squeeze the loop with pliers to tighten.

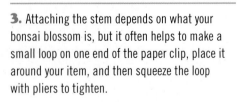

MIXED-UP BONSAI

COMPUTER
KEYS

COSTUME
JEWELRY

FISHING
LURES

41

PLANT a COLLECTIBLE GARDEN

Garbage Flower arrangements are the perfect way to display small collections: baseball cards, costume jewelry, toy cars, toy soldiers, etc.

SINGLE PRECIOUS ITEM

A single or sentimental item, like a lone earring or a charm, makes a lovely Garbage Flower.

DOLL HOUSE FAMILY COLLECTION

MAERSK SEALAND

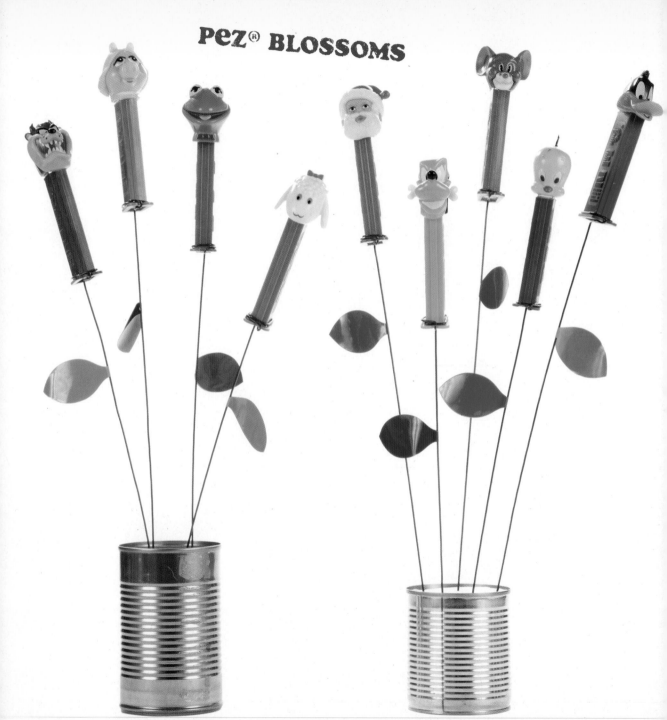

PEZ® BLOSSOMS

GLASS MENAGERIE MINI
Better than a grandma shelf!

GROW a GARDEN OF YOU:
YOUR LIFE IN
GARBAGE FLOWERS

Put yourself on display with a 3-D autobiographical arrangement.

eric as baby, wow!

eric's favorite car

GROW a travel-tanical GARDEN

Finally, there's something artful to do with the stuff you collect while you travel—the bits that don't fit in the photo album and are too lumpy for the scrapbook! Create an arrangement around one trip with individual flowers made from everything from drink coasters and maps to matchbooks and gorgeous foreign money. Or use something exotic (and not too expensive) from the mini-bar. Make a bigger arrangement that represents your worldwide adventures and add to it each time you come home.

HOW TO RECYCLE THIS BOOK INTO 3 GARBAGE FLOWERS

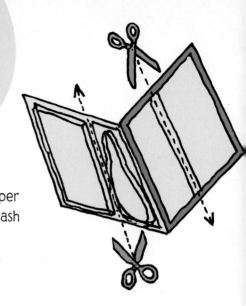

1. Tear the plastic case at the front of the book from the front cover. Don't worry if orange paper stays stuck to the plastic case. This will add a dash of color to the bouquet.

Cut away the larger rectangles that held the stem wire on both sides of the case.

2. Cut the resulting shape, perpendicular to the case's hinge, into three equal-ish shapes.

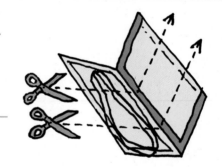

WRAP WIRE AROUND SPINE

3. Wrap stem wires around the hinges, using the pliers to pinch it tightly to the plastic.

4. Add leaves, and plant this book! Ta-daaa!